Teri
the Trampolining
Fairy

By Daisy Meadows

ORCHARD

www.rainbowmagicbooks.co.uk

The Fairyland Palace

Fairy Arena

Tippington Town

Cool Kids Leisure Centre

Teri
the Trampolining
Fairy

Join the **Rainbow Magic Reading Challenge!**

Read the story and collect your fairy points to climb the

To the children of Stoke Fleming Primary School

Special thanks to
Rachel Elliot

ORCHARD BOOKS

First published in Great Britain in 2019 by The Watts Publishing Group

1 3 5 7 9 10 8 6 4 2

© 2019 Rainbow Magic Limited.
© 2019 HIT Entertainment Limited.
Illustrations © Orchard Books 2019

HIT entertainment

The moral rights of the author and illustrator have been asserted.

A CIP catalogue record for this book is available from the British Library.

ISBN 978 1 40835 520 6

Printed and bound in Great Britain by Clays Ltd, Elcograf S.p.A

MIX
Paper from
responsible sources
FSC® C104740

The paper and board used in this book are made from wood from responsible sources

Orchard Books
An imprint of Hachette Children's Group
Part of The Watts Publishing Group Limited
Carmelite House, 50 Victoria Embankment, London EC4Y 0DZ

An Hachette UK Company
www.hachette.co.uk
www.hachettechildrens.co.uk

Jack Frost's Spell

I must get strong! I'll start today.
But kids are getting in my way.
They jump and run, they spin and bound.
I can't do sports with them around!

Goblins, ruin every club.
Spoil their sports and make them blub.
I'll prove it's true, for all to see:
My sister's not as strong as me!

Contents

Chapter One
Ice Cool

"There she is!" Rachel Walker cried in excitement. "Kirsty! Kirsty!"

She jumped out of her dad's car, waving to her best friend. Kirsty Tate waved back.

"Isn't this brilliant?" said Kirsty, running up to Rachel and hugging her.

"Now there's a leisure centre halfway between our homes, we can go to the same after-school club."

"I love sharing things with you," said Rachel, winking at Kirsty.

Kirsty winked back. She knew that Rachel was talking about their most precious secret. Their friendship was truly magical, because it had grown stronger with each adventure they shared as friends of Fairyland.

The girls looked up at the sign hanging over the door.

"Cool Kids Leisure Centre," Rachel read aloud. "I can't wait to see inside and choose a club."

"How are we going to decide?" asked Kirsty.

"There are taster classes for each of the

clubs," said Mr Tate. "When you've tried them all out, you can choose which one you like best."

"Go and have fun," said Mr Walker. "We're going to try out the new gym, so we'll see you later."

Rachel and Kirsty picked up their sports bags and hurried into the leisure

centre. Inside, a young woman jogged over to meet them.

"Hi, I'm Lucy," she said. "Welcome to Ice Cool! Are you here for the after-school club taster sessions?"

The girls nodded.

"This place looks amazing," said Rachel, gazing around. Everything was gleaming and new.

"Thanks," said Lucy with a smile.

"Have you had lots of customers?" Kirsty asked.

Lucy's smile faded a little.

"Not so far," she said. "I'm hoping that the after-school clubs will get more people talking about us. Here's a list of all the different clubs. What do you want to try first?"

"Ooh, let's start with the trampolining

club," said Rachel. "That sounds like fun."

Lucy added their names to her list.

"The changing rooms are just down there," she said, pointing. "When you're ready, make your way into hall one. And have fun!"

As soon as the girls were ready, they put their bags into a locker and made their way to hall one. Several trampolines had been set up, and children were already bouncing on them. A redheaded woman beckoned them over.

"Welcome to the class," she said. "I'm Edie, and I am the trampolining teacher. Let's get you started. Before you do any bouncing, you need to warm up."

Edie led the girls through some simple stretches. As they were touching their toes, there was a huge crash and a yell. One of the trampolines had collapsed.

"Oh my goodness," Edie cried, running over to the trampoline. "Is everyone OK?"

A boy clambered off the trampoline.

"I'm fine," he said. "I don't know what happened. It just folded under me."

Edie crouched down and looked under the trampoline.

"The legs have fallen off," she said. "How could this have happened? I checked them all before the class and they were fine."

"At least there are other trampolines we can use," said Rachel.

She climbed up on to the next trampoline and jumped.

"Ouch!" she exclaimed. "It's not bouncy at all."

Edie put her hand on the trampoline and frowned.

"It's hard," she said in amazement. "Everyone, I'm sorry, but you will have to go and take a break while I try to work out what's going on."

"Let's get a drink of water," Kirsty suggested.

The girls went to the water cooler at

the far end of the hall. Kirsty reached out and took a cup.

"That's a pretty cup," Rachel said. "It's shimmering like a mother-of-pearl shell."

Kirsty put the cup under the water cooler tap and pressed the button. Instead of water, a stream of rainbow colours poured into the cup, glittering with magic. The girls shared a delighted smile as a tiny fairy popped up out of the colour swirl. There were swirls all over her pink sports kit too, and a few glowing ribbons of

fairy dust twirled around her neat bun of black hair.

"Rachel, Kirsty, thank goodness I found you," she said, gasping. "I'm Teri the Trampolining Fairy, and I've come to ask for your help."

"Of course," said Rachel at once. "Let's

find somewhere private so we can talk."

"The cubicles in the changing rooms," said Kirsty. "Come on!"

The girls hurried back to the changing room with the shining cup. They squeezed into a single cubicle, and Rachel sat on the bench while Kirsty stood with her back to the door. Then Teri sprang out of the cup.

"How can we help?" asked Rachel at once.

Chapter Two
Fairyland Arena

Teri landed on Kirsty's palm with her hands on her hips.

"Jack Frost has done the most terrible thing, and I don't know how to put it right," she blurted out. "You see, I'm one of the After School Sports Fairies. Each of us has a magical bracelet, and we use them to watch over after-school sports clubs. We make sure that the equipment works and nothing stops the children from having fun."

"That sounds like a lovely job," said Kirsty, smiling.

"It is," Teri agreed. "I look after the trampolining clubs. I love getting the children bouncing and having fun! But now Jack Frost has put a stop to our good work. He has stolen our bracelets and hidden them from us."

"Jack Frost loves to spoil people's fun," said Rachel. "Teri, I promise we will do everything we can to help get your bracelets back."

"I thought Jack Frost was fed up with sports," said Kirsty. "After we helped the Sporty Fairies to stop him spoiling the

Fairyland Olympics, he stomped off in a temper."

"He hasn't bothered any of the Sporty Fairies again," said Teri. "But last week he lost an arm-wrestling competition to his sister, Jilly Chilly. Now he has decided that he has to get fit so he can beat her.

But he doesn't want anyone to see him exercising, and he's planning to use our bracelets to help him somehow."

"Whatever he's planning, you can be sure it's something mean," said Kirsty. "If Jack Frost can find a way to cheat at something, he'll do it."

"Will you come to Fairyland with me?" Teri asked. "We don't know what to do next."

The girls nodded, feeling the thrill of excitement they always got when they were about to turn into fairies.

Teri waved her wand. *BOING!* A golden flash of fairy magic hit the floor of the cubicle and sprang up around them. At the same moment, the girls began to bounce. They were small bounces at first, but each one got higher and higher. And with every bounce, the girls felt themselves growing smaller. Soon they were the same size as Teri, and their delicate fairy wings were carrying them even higher.

"This is wonderful," said Rachel, somersaulting over the cubicle door.

Kirsty somersaulted after her. Then Teri held out her wand and drew a glimmering circle of light in the air.

"This way," she called. "Fairyland is waiting for you!"

The changing room disappeared as soon as Rachel and Kirsty somersaulted through the circle of light. They landed on their feet in the middle of a round, open space. There were rows of seats all around them.

"We've been here before," said Kirsty, looking at the rows of empty seats all around them. "This is the Fairyland Arena."

The last time the girls had been to the arena was to watch the Fairyland

Olympics. The seats had been filled with
cheering fairies, elves, pixies and goblins.
Flags and banners had filled the air,
changing colour and playing tunes. It
was very different today.

"It seems so quiet," said Rachel.

"Not for long," said Teri, laughing.
"Here come the others."

Three fairies were speeding towards

them, waving and smiling. They landed
and threw their arms around Rachel and
Kirsty.

"You're here!" they cried. "You really
came! Thank you!"

"Let me introduce everyone," said Teri,

giving a little bounce of excitement. "This is Bonnie the Bike-Riding Fairy, that's Rita the Rollerskating Fairy whizzing around in circles, and this is Callie the Climbing Fairy, who climbs more often than she flies!"

"Are you always this full of energy?" Rachel asked, laughing as Rita zoomed past.

"We're usually much bouncier than this," said Teri.

"We need plenty of energy because we have so much to do," said Callie. "We make sure that classes run on time, teachers are healthy, equipment works well, children learn and remember what they have been taught, and everyone has lots of fun."

"It's our job to help children pour their

fizzy energy into after-school sports,"
added Bonnie. "But without our bracelets,
after-school clubs everywhere will start
going horribly wrong. We have to find
out what Jack Frost has done with them."

"How did he get them?" said Kirsty.

Rita spun around on her rollerskates
and flicked her wand upwards. A large
video screen appeared above the arena.

"Our magical sports camera records
everything that goes on at the arena," she
explained. "Luckily, that means we can
show you exactly what happened."

Chapter Three
A Frosty Trampoline

Rachel and Kirsty watched the screen
flicker into life. It showed a row of lockers
in every colour of the rainbow. Suddenly,
Jack Frost crept into the shot. He looked
around with a sly expression. Then he
rubbed his hands together and pointed
his wand at a pink locker.

"That's mine," said Teri in a miserable voice.

The locker door swung open and Jack Frost's hand darted inside. He pulled out a small, glittering bracelet and fastened it around his wrist. Then he pointed his wand at the next locker.

"That's mine," said Rita, as the next door opened.

One by one, Jack Frost broke into the lockers and put all the beautiful bracelets on his wrist. Then he gave a twirl and cackled with laughter.

"Now I can finally get what I want," he said. "All that after-school energy will

make me fitter than Jilly Chilly. Then I'll
teach her a lesson!"

There was a bright flash of blue
lightning, and the Ice Lord had vanished.
The picture on the screen faded away.

"I wonder where he went," said Rachel.
"Maybe his Ice Castle, or Goblin Grotto."

"He might have gone straight back
to the castle to see Jilly Chilly," Kirsty
suggested.

"Let's follow him," said Teri, jumping up
and down.

"But what are we going to do when
we get there?" asked Rachel. "How are
we going to find the bracelets?"

"I don't know," said Teri. "But I do
know that my magic works best when I
haven't made a plan. Let's just bounce up
to the castle and see what happens!"

Rachel and Kirsty exchanged a worried glance.

"Jack Frost's Castle can be a dangerous place for fairies," said Rachel.

"We'll all be there to protect each other," said Teri, smiling. "Besides, I bet that a plan will pop up as soon as we get there."

The four After School Sports Fairies bounded into the air, twirling, spinning, somersaulting and back-flipping.

"No time to waste!" they cried. "Let's go!"

Rachel and Kirsty zoomed along with them towards Jack Frost's Castle.

"I feel as if they're sweeping us up, like a strong, magical wave," said Kirsty.

"You're right. And a strong, magical wave sounds like just what we need to defeat Jack Frost," said Rachel.

Soon, the rich colours of Fairyland started to fade, and the air turned icy. The forest below was blurred under a thick layer of fog.

"Listen," said Teri, stopping suddenly and holding up her hand. "Can you hear that?"

They all listened. At first, they couldn't hear anything. Then, out of the silence, came a faint noise.

BOING!

BOING! BOING!

"It's a trampoline," said Teri. "I'd know that sound anywhere. Come on!"

They fluttered down slowly. The fog blinded them, but the bouncing noises led the way. At last they felt the scrunch of snow beneath their feet.

"We've landed," Rita whispered. "What now?"

Between the fog and the shadows of the forest, they couldn't even see each other's faces.

"It's like being blindfolded," said
Rachel.

"Let's all hold hands," said Kirsty. "It
would be easy to lose each other in here."

Hand in hand, the six fairies walked
towards the sound of the trampoline.
Kirsty led the way slowly, holding out her
free hand to stop herself from bumping
into tree trunks.

"I think I can see a light ahead," she
said.

After a few more steps, the fairies found themselves in a little clearing. Three goblins were standing around the glade, and each one was holding a torch. None of them noticed the fairies. They were too busy shining the light under their chins to scare each other.

A trampoline mat had been stretched between four trees, and Jack Frost was bouncing on it.

"Woohoo!" he

shouted as he rocketed upwards.

"Wheeee!" he shrieked as he hurtled downwards.

"Yikes!" he yelled as he bounced sideways. "How do you work this thing?"

"I knew I'd heard a trampoline," said Teri. "Oh my goodness, look."

Jack Frost was still wearing all four magical bracelets around his wrist.

Chapter Four
An Icy Warning

"Argh!" Jack Frost bellowed.

This time he had bounced a little too high, and hit three branches on the way down. He landed on his back in the middle of the trampoline.

"Whose stupid idea was it to put the trampoline in the woods?" he roared, yanking twigs out of his beard.

"Yours," said all the goblins together.

"Shut up," Jack Frost snarled. "And stop looking at me! I need a proper place to exercise. The ceilings in the castle are too low for bouncing. I need my own leisure centre. You goblins must build me one!"

"We can't," the goblins wailed. "We don't know how!"

"Yes, anything you build would probably fall down," Jack Frost muttered. "Wait! I have a better idea. There is a new leisure centre in the human world that would be perfect. It's even named after me – Cool! All you nincompoops need to do is spoil their classes and they will have to close down. Then it will be all mine. I am a genius!"

Rachel couldn't bear to listen any

more. She broke away from the other fairies and ran into the clearing.

"Go away, pesky fairy!" one of the goblins shouted.

Rachel ignored him and spoke to Jack Frost instead.

"You can't spoil this for everyone," she cried. "That would just be selfish."

"Don't you know me yet?" Jack Frost jeered. "Selfish is my middle name."

Yanking the first bracelet from his wrist, he flung it at the nearest goblin. With a bright blue flash, the goblin and the bracelet completely disappeared.

"Go, my gormless goblins, and wreck the new leisure centre," Jack Frost shouted. "Confuse the classes and spoil the sports. Make sure that no one wants to be there! Then I can exercise in peace and beat Jilly Chilly – with my magical bracelets!"

"Stop!" Rachel cried.

Kirsty and the other fairies flew out from the trees to join her.

Jack Frost flung a bracelet at the second goblin, and another at the third. They both disappeared.

"Follow those bracelets!" Teri exclaimed.

There was a sudden flurry of fairy dust, and Callie, Rita and Bonnie vanished from the clearing.

"You won't get this one either," said Jack Frost, holding up his wrist with the last bracelet gleaming on it. "It will stay in the heart of my Ice Castle. Give up, feeble fairies!"

With a deafening crack of thunder, Jack Frost was gone. Teri buried her face in her hands.

"We'll never get my bracelet back," whispered. "We can't take it from the heart of the Ice Castle."

"Oh, can't we?" said Rachel in a bold voice. "We'll see about that. Kirsty and I have been into the Ice Castle plenty of times. He can't keep us out."

Kirsty put her arm around Teri's shoulders and gave her a friendly squeeze.

"We can do it," she said. "Come on –

let's fly to the castle and find a way in."

The fog had wrapped itself around the Ice Castle too. Only the very tips of the six towers could be seen. Even the chilly battlements were hidden.

"This fog might help us," said Rachel. "We can fly close and peep through the windows without being seen."

Teri dipped her wand into the fog, and drew out a thin thread of mist. As the girls watched, the thread knitted itself into three cosy cloaks.

"Put these on," said Teri. "While we're wrapped in fog, the goblin guards won't be able to spot us."

Wearing their frothy white cloaks, the fairies flew closer to the castle.

"Look up," said Kirsty suddenly.

It was one of the oddest sights they had ever seen. From the top of the castle, goblin guards were leaping and bouncing out of the fog – sometimes upside down,

sometimes on their backs – and all cackling and squawking with laughter before they vanished into the fog again.

"They must have trampolines on the battlements," said Rachel, stifling a giggle. "I don't think they're going to notice us."

The fairies peeped through the first window. They could see a goblin doing star jumps on a small trampoline.

"Let's try the next one," said Teri.

The next window was open, and the room was empty. The

fairies slipped inside and their misty
cloaks melted away.

"I don't think we need to worry about
being quiet," said Kirsty.

The castle was ringing with squawks,
shouts and wails. The fairies fluttered out
of the room into the corridor, and found
that it was crammed full of trampolines.
Goblins were staggering across them,
tripping over them and crawling
underneath them. Stranger still, some of
the trampolines were moving. They were
crawling along like enormous, colourful
beetles.

"I'm stuck!" yelled one.

"I'm tangled in a trampoline!" squealed
another.

The fairies swooped up out of sight.

"Why on earth are the trampolines

moving?" asked Kirsty in amazement.

"This is one of the strangest things
I have ever seen," said Rachel, as a
trampoline rose up on its legs and leaned
against the wall. "What has Jack Frost
been doing?"

"He has no idea how to use my magic

properly," said Teri. "Come on, let's follow the trampolines. They might lead us to Jack Frost and my bracelet."

It was easy to follow Jack Frost's trail. Large and small, the trampolines scurried along the corridors. They were piled up in doorways and jammed into cupboards. At the end of one particularly jumbled-up corridor, the fairies came to a large, wooden door. From inside, they could hear a faint, scratchy voice

"Listen," said Kirsty. "I think Jack Frost is singing."

Chapter Five
Jack Frost Plays a Trick

The fairies pressed their ears against the door. The singing was clearer now.

"*I beat the fairies, ha ha ha!*
They're so stupid, hee hee hee!
I played a funny game, tra la la!
No one here is as clever as me!"

"Shall we go in?" asked Teri.

Rachel and Kirsty took a deep breath
and nodded. Rachel reached out to turn
the door handle, but she never touched it.
From behind them, there came the sound
of panting and scrambling. A goblin leapt
down from a tower of trampolines, pelted
towards the door and burst through
it, leaving a goblin-shaped hole in the
wood. Rachel, Kirsty and Teri peered

through the hole.

"Oh my goodness, it's a bathroom!"
said Rachel.

Jack Frost was sitting in a bubble bath,
holding a long-handled back scrubber.
He was wearing a blue shower cap,
decorated with silver polka dots, and he
was staring at the goblin with his mouth
wide open. The goblin had jumped into
the bath opposite him, and was wearing

a white bubble beard.

"What are you doing?" Jack Frost yelled. "Get out!"

"I'm scared of the trampolines," the goblin wailed. "And I'm scared of the fairies!"

"I gave some of them legs so they could move out of my way," Jack Frost snapped. "Hang on – what fairies?"

The goblin cringed and pointed at the doorway. Jack Frost whipped around and glared at Teri, Rachel and Kirsty.

"You!" he said, pointing at Teri. "Get rid of all these trampolines. I never wanted this many."

"You started this by stealing my bracelet," said Teri. "Give it back to me."

"It's not here," said Jack Frost, showing her his bare wrists. "Get rid of the

trampolines and then you can have your
bracelet."

"I can't," said Teri, truthfully. "Without
my bracelet, I can't control the
trampoline magic."

"Fine," said Jack Frost through
gritted teeth. "Everyone, get out of my
bathroom!"

The goblin was pushed
out of the bubbles, and
he squelched away past
the fairies. They watched
him edge around the
piled-up trampolines.
At that moment, Jack
Frost appeared in the
bathroom doorway. He
was wrapped in a flowery
towel with a turban

around his head.

"I'll have to take you to the bracelet,"
he said in a grumpy voice. "It's in such
an amazing hiding place that you'll
never find it. No one is as good as me at
finding hiding places."

He led the three fairies along the
corridor. They went down first one
staircase and then another, deep into the
Ice Castle. At last he pointed towards a
narrow staircase made of ice.

"Down there," he said.

The fairies fluttered down the stairs,
shivering. At the bottom of the staircase
was a blank wall.

"There's nothing here," said Kirsty.

"It's a secret room," Jack Frost hissed.
"You have to say, 'Ice is nice' to reveal
the door."

The three fairies said the words together, and at once the blank wall seemed to melt away. They saw a small room behind a large metal gate. The bracelet lay in the middle of the room.

"At last!" cried Teri.

Jack Frost stomped down the steps and took out a key. As soon as the gate was unlocked, Teri darted into the room to pick up the bracelet. As Rachel and Kirsty took a step forward to see it, the Ice Lord shoved them aside and snatched Teri's wand.

"As if I'd ever give the bracelet back!"

he shouted, slamming and locking the gate.

"Let us out!" Rachel cried, grabbing the bars and shaking them.

But Jack Frost turned and raced back up the steps. The three fairies exchanged looks of alarm.

"We're stuck inside a secret room in Jack Frost's dungeon with no wand," said Kirsty. "How are we ever going to get out?"

Teri sank to the cold floor.

"Can't we use your magical bracelet?" asked Rachel.

Teri shook her head.

"Its magic is only for trampolining," she explained. "It can't get us out of a locked room."

"Maybe it can," said Kirsty in an

excited voice, smiling at her friends.

She knelt down and pushed on the bottom of one of the bars. It gave a very tiny wobble.

"It's loose," said Rachel. "But how does that help us? It's not loose enough for us to pull it out."

"But maybe it's loose enough for a little bounce," said Kirsty.

Chapter Six
The Goblin Rumpus

Teri slipped the bracelet on to her wrist and held it against the loose bar. For a moment, nothing happened. Then the bar began to glow, and gave a tiny bounce. Then a slightly bigger bounce . . . and another . . . until at last the bar bounced straight out of the gate.

"Hurray!" the fairies cheered.

It was a narrow gap, but they all managed to squeeze through.

"Now, let's go and find your magic wand," said Kirsty.

"Yes," said Teri with a smile. "Then I can take this bracelet back to the Fairyland Arena where it belongs."

The three fairies flew up the staircases and out of the dungeon.

"Keep looking out for goblins," said Rachel.

Strangely, there was not a single goblin to be seen. However, there was a deafening rumpus coming from the throne room. Squawks, shrieks, wails and whoops echoed down the corridors.

"Let's see what's going on," said Kirsty, darting ahead.

When she reached the door, she pushed it open a little way and peeked through the gap.

"Oh dear," she said.

"What is it?" asked Rachel.

Kirsty let the door swing open.

"Be careful not to be seen," Teri said.

"I don't think it matters at this moment," Kirsty replied.

The throne room was in utter chaos. Trampolines were floating in the air. Goblins were running around in circles, some with skunks' tails, some with hairy legs, and one with a horse's mane all the way down his back. There was a group of pink, yellow and red goblins yelling at each other beside the throne. Pine cones with wings and unicorn horns were fluttering through the air, bumping into goblins, each other and the walls. Jack Frost was nowhere to be seen,

"There!" cried Rachel.

She pointed to the window, where two goblins were having a tug of war with Teri's wand.

"Jack Frost has let the goblins play with my wand," Teri said with a groan. "We have to get it back before they do any more damage."

At that moment, one of the goblins shouted, "ABRACADABRA!" and the throne room was filled with tiny fireworks. The goblins squawked and dived under the furniture.

"We have to get Teri's wand back before the goblins destroy everything," Rachel shouted over the noise.

"We can do it," said Kirsty. "Let's go!"

Dodging fireworks, enchanted pine cones and flying trampolines, the best friends zigzagged across the throne room.

The goblins with the wand were both hiding under the same small table, their green bottoms sticking out and quivering. Carefully, Rachel and Kirsty lifted the table. The goblins had their eyes tightly shut and their fingers in their ears. They didn't seem to notice that their shelter had been taken away.

"Look, one of them is kneeling on the wand," Rachel exclaimed.

"Let's each take one side," said Kirsty.

Very, very slowly, she and Rachel tried to pull the wand out from under the goblin's knee, but it wouldn't budge.

"He's too heavy," Rachel whispered.

Kirsty looked at Teri, who winked at her.

"How about just one more bounce?" she said.

Gently, she brushed her bracelet against the goblin's bony knees. They started to glow, and the glow spread quickly up and down his legs. Then . . . *BOING!* Like an enormous frog, the goblin sprang into the air.

"Yikes!" the goblin wailed.

Rachel picked up the wand and then handed it to Teri. With a few quick flicks, the fireworks and trampolines had vanished, the pinecones were gathered in neat piles on the floor and the goblins were back to their normal selves.

"Thank you both," said Teri, flinging her arms around them and jumping up and down. "Now we can celebrate!"

"You're welcome," said Kirsty, laughing. "But maybe we should get away from here first?"

"I wonder what Jack Frost will do when he realises we've escaped," said Rachel.

Just then, a furious roar echoed through the castle, and the icy walls shook.

"Oh my goodness, let's not wait around to find out," said Teri. "I'll send you straight back to the leisure centre.

Hopefully you will see the other fairies there – and you should be able to enjoy a bit of trampolining too!"

She flicked her wand, and the girls felt something pick them up and spin them around. When they stopped feeling dizzy, the throne room had completely disappeared.

"We're back in the changing cubicle at the Cool Kids Leisure Centre," said Kirsty in wonder.

"And I'll bet not a single second has passed since we went to Fairyland," said Rachel, smiling.

Just then there was a knock at the cubicle door.

"Girls, are you in there?" came Edie's voice. "I have good news: the trampolines are working again. Are you ready to do some bouncing?"

"We're ready," said Kirsty, reaching out to open the door. "Ready to jump right in to our next adventure!"

The End

**Now it's time for Kirsty and
Rachel to help ...**

Bonnie the Bike-Riding Fairy

Read on for a sneak peek ...

Rachel Walker did ten star jumps and
then cartwheeled across the foyer of the
Cool Kids Leisure Centre.

"That was so much fun," she said to her
best friend, Kirsty Tate.

"Yes, I can't stop smiling," Kirsty said.
"I didn't expect to like trampolining so
much!"

"Thank goodness we were able to help
Teri the Trampolining Fairy find her
bracelet," said Rachel.

Earlier that day, Teri had whisked
them off to Fairyland, where they had
met the After-School Sports Fairies. The

fairies were very upset because naughty Jack Frost had stolen their magical bracelets. He wanted to get fit so that he could beat his sister Jilly Chilly at arm-wrestling, but he didn't want anyone to see him training. He planned to use the magical bracelets to ruin all after-school sports clubs. Then he would have the leisure centre to himself, where he could train all on his own. Rachel and Kirsty had promised to help return the bracelets to their rightful owners.

"I hope we can find the other bracelets soon," said Rachel. "If all the clubs are as much fun as trampolining, it would be awful if Jack Frost spoiled them."

"Do you want to pick trampolining for our after-school sports club?" Kirsty asked.

"Let's try the other trial classes first," said Rachel, laughing. "What's next?"

"There's Lucy," said Kirsty, noticing the young woman who had signed them up for the trial classes. "Let's ask her."

Lucy smiled when she saw them.

Read Bonnie the Bike-Riding Fairy to find out what adventures are in store for Kirsty and Rachel!

Calling all parents, carers and teachers!
The Rainbow Magic fairies are here to help
your child enter the magical world of reading.
Whatever reading stage they are at, there's
a Rainbow Magic book for everyone!
Here is Lydia the Reading Fairy's guide to
supporting your child's journey at all levels.

Starting Out

Our Rainbow Magic Beginner Readers are perfect for first-time readers who are just beginning to develop reading skills and confidence. Approved by teachers, they contain a full range of educational levelling, as well as lively full-colour illustrations.

Developing Readers

Rainbow Magic Early Readers contain longer stories and wider vocabulary for building stamina and growing confidence. These are adaptations of our most popular Rainbow Magic stories, specially developed for younger readers in conjunction with an Early Years reading consultant, with full-colour illustrations.

Going Solo

The Rainbow Magic chapter books – a mixture of series and one-off specials – contain accessible writing to encourage your child to venture into reading independently. These highly collectible and much-loved magical stories inspire a love of reading to last a lifetime.

www.rainbowmagicbooks.co.uk

"Rainbow Magic got my daughter reading chapter books. Great sparkly covers, cute fairies and traditional stories full of magic that she found impossible to put down" - Mother of Edie (6 years)

"Florence LOVES the Rainbow Magic books. She really enjoys reading now" - Mother of Florence (6 years)

Read along the Reading Rainbow!

Well done – you have completed the book!

This book was worth 1 star.

See how far you have climbed on the Reading Rainbow opposite.
The more books you read, the more stars you can colour in
and the closer you will be to becoming a Royal Fairy!

Do you want to print your own Reading Rainbow?

1) Go to the Rainbow Magic website

2) Download and print out the poster

3) Colour in a star for every book you finish
and climb the Reading Rainbow

4) For every step up the rainbow,
you can download your very own certificate

There's all this and lots more at
rainbowmagicbooks.co.uk

You'll find activities, stories, a special newsletter
AND you can search for the fairy with your name!